IS GOD STILL AWAKE?

A SMALL GIRL WITH A BIG QUESTION ABOUT GOD

SHEILA WALSH

ILLUSTRATED BY ALEKSANDRA SZMIDT

Tommy NELSON

An Imprint of Thomas Nelson

Published in Nashville, Tennessee, by Tommy Nelson. Tommy Nelson is an imprint of Thomas Nelson. Thomas Nelson is a registered trademark of HarperCollins Christian Publishing, Inc.

Tommy Nelson titles may be purchased in bulk for educational, business, fund-raising, or sales promotional use. For information, please email SpecialMarkets@ThomasNelson.com.

Scripture quotations marked ICB are taken from the International Children's Bible®. Copyright © 1986, 1988, 1999, 2015 by Thomas Nelson. Used by permission. All rights reserved.

ISBN 978-1-4002-2964-2 (eBook)
ISBN 978-1-4002-2963-5 (HC)
ISBN 978-1-4002-3384-7 (IE)

Library of Congress Cataloging-in-Publication Data

Names: Walsh, Sheila, 1956- author. | Szmidt, Aleksandra, illustrator.
Title: 1s God still awake? : a small girl with a big question about God / Sheila Walsh ; illustrated by Aleksandra Szmidt.
Description: Nashville, Tennessee : Thomas Nelson, [2021] | Audience: Ages 4-8 | Summary: "In her first children's book about prayer, Is God Still Awake?, bestselling author Sheila Walsh helps you teach your child about God and the incredible ways we can spend time with Him at any moment"-- Provided by publisher.
Identifiers: LCCN 2021019738 (print) | LCCN 2021019739 (ebook) | ISBN 9781400229635 (h/c) | ISBN 9781400229659 (bb) | ISBN 9781400233847 (ie) | ISBN 9781400229642 (ebook)
Subjects: LCSH: Prayer--Christianity--Juvenile literature. | BISAC: JUVENILE FICTION / Religious / Christian / Emotions & Feelings | JUVENILE FICTION / Religious / Christian / Humorous
Classification: LCC BV212 .W35 2021 (print) | LCC BV212 (ebook) | DDC 248.3/2083--dc23
LC record available at https://lccn.loc.gov/2021019738
LC ebook record available at https://lccn.loc.gov/2021019739

Written by Sheila Walsh

Illustrated by Aleksandra Szmidt

Printed in Malaysia

21 22 23 24 25   IMG   10 9 8 7 6 5 4 3 2 1

Mfr: IMG / Singapore, Republic of Singapore / October 2021 / PO #12040398

This book is dedicated with love to every little one in this great big world who has ever wondered, *Does God see me?*

—Sheila Walsh

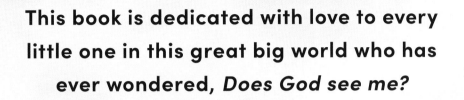

For my mother and father. Thank you for a happy childhood—a constant source of inspiration for my work.

—Aleksandra Szmidt

My name is **Poppy**,
and I may be small,

but I have a **big** question,
the **biggest of all.**

Is God always with me,
or does He take a break?

When I go to sleep,
is God still awake?

And when I wake up,
is God awake too?

Is He watching me then?
Is God watching **you?**

Does God hear a whisper,
or do we have to **shout?**

Will you join my **adventure**
and help me
find out?

Is God always there
when the sun hits my head
and Mom and Dad call me
to get out of bed?

But I'm **comfy** and **cozy**
and I want to stay.

My fluffy cat, Pat, feels **just the same way.**

Then I hop
down the stairs,
taking two at a time.

Someone's tummy is
rumbling—
I don't think it's mine.

When we sit down
for breakfast,
I think God's awake.
'Cause He hears us
say thank you . . .
and the noises
Ben makes.

Most of Ben's food
ends up on the floor,

where Noodle the poodle is
waiting for more.

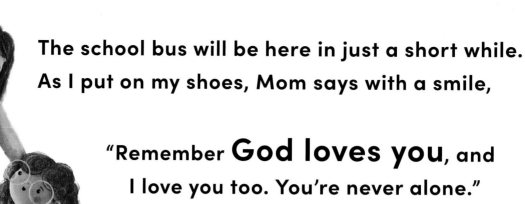

The school bus will be here in just a short while.
As I put on my shoes, Mom says with a smile,

"Remember **God loves you**, and
I love you too. You're never alone."

I think that's
a clue!

So I wait for the bus
with my panda lunch box.

Does God see that too?
Can He hear all my thoughts?

When I dream up a world where puppies are blue
and ponies are purple, **does God see that too?**

At school we are learning about **numbers** and **shapes**
and how many letters an alphabet takes.

For art, I am painting a silly green dog.
My teacher, Miss Crump, says, **"Oh, what a cute frog!"**

As I learn and I grow,
does God really see
all the ways I'm becoming
who I'm going to be?

My friend **Isabella**
is one of a kind.

She joins my adventure
to see what we'll find.

We agree God's awake
when we're running around
and pretending to be
superheroes who
rescue
the crowd.

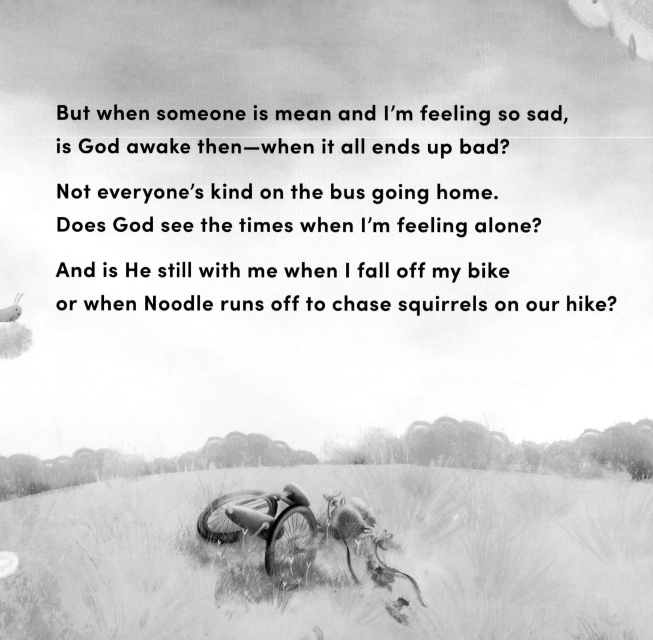

But when someone is mean and I'm feeling so sad,
is God awake then—when it all ends up bad?

Not everyone's kind on the bus going home.
Does God see the times when I'm feeling alone?

And is He still with me when I fall off my bike
or when Noodle runs off to chase squirrels on our hike?

I remember what Mom says about

God's great love.

Perhaps He cares more than I ever dreamed of.

I can lie on the grass
and look up at the sky.
I can feel **God is with me**,
right there by my side.

When everything's quiet
and I'm all on my own,
can I talk to God then,
like I talk on the phone?

If I'm feeling afraid
for no reason
at all,
is God
awake
then?

Will He
answer
my call?

Is God watching me when
I'm good or I'm bad?

**Can I pray
when I'm happy?
Can I pray
when I'm sad?**

Or what if I do something wrong
by mistake—
like I run through the kitchen,
knocking over the cake?

My mom had been baking
for such a long time.
Now the cake's inside Noodle,
but he seems just fine.

We go for a walk
before bed every day.
As the sun disappears,
I hear Daddy say,
"Thank You, dear God,
for all that You do."

Dad believes that
God hears him
and that God
hears me too.

And when we get home
and I'm all dressed for bed
and Noodle's asleep
chasing cats in his head,

z z z...

Dad opens my Bible and reads about how
God's never asleep—
He's awake even now.
The psalm says He'll help us and watch over us.
The Bible says so many things I can trust.

Now I know **God is listening**
to the prayers that I pray
while Pat, my big cat,
does her evening ballet.

When Mom and Dad kiss me
and tell me good night,
they say God is with me
as they turn off the light.

With **Noodle** and **Pat,**
I'm tucked into bed
and thinking about
what my dad and I read.

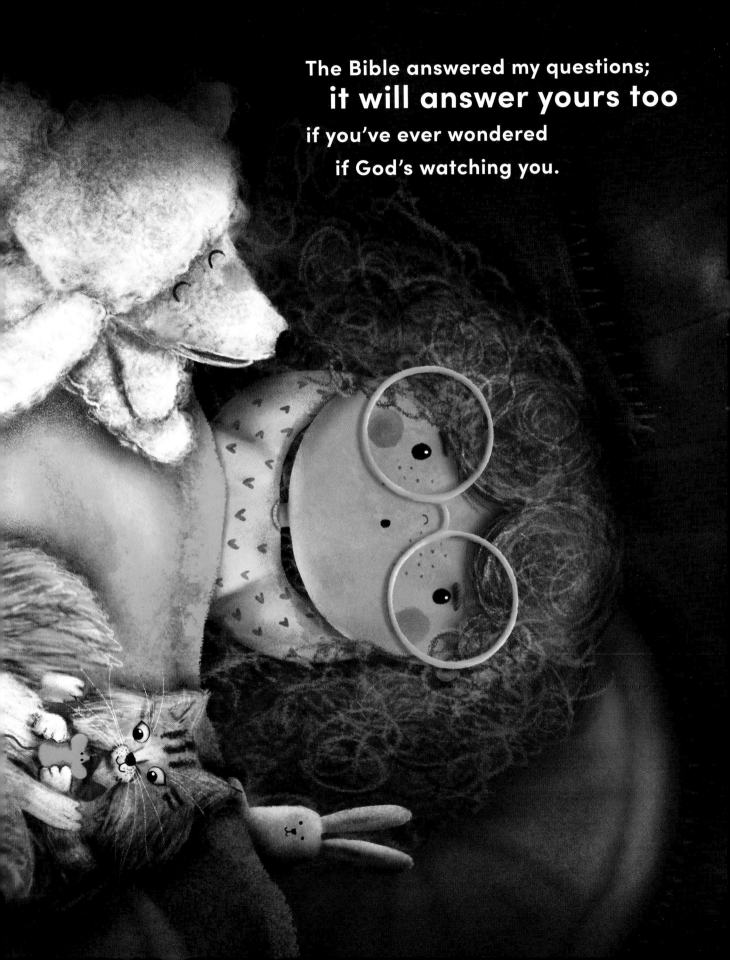

The Bible answered my questions;
it will answer yours too
if you've ever wondered
if God's watching you.

Now here's the **big** answer,
and it's truly the best:
**God never sleeps.
He never
needs rest.**
God is always awake,
so I'm **never alone.**
He's with me at school.
He's with me at home.

He's there with you too—
every night, every day.
He's listening now, so
**take a moment
to say . . .**

God, I know that
You're with me.

I believe that You're near.

You won't fall asleep.
**I don't
have to fear.**
Thank You for hearing
and loving me too.

What I want to say most is
I really
love You.

I look up to the hills.
But where does
my help come from?
My help comes from the Lord.
He made heaven and earth.
He will not let you be defeated.
He who guards you never sleeps.

PSALM 121:1–3 ICB